TO MY DANCE PARTNER IN LIFE, SHELDON,
AND TO ALL THE LITTLE DANCERS IN THE WORLD,
ESPECIALLY OUR NIECES, ZORAH AND ANYAH.

−VB

LET GO, DANCE, FLOW, ENJOY. FOR YOU.

−MD

Boyds Mills Press
An imprint of Boyds Mills & Kane,
a division of Astra Publishing House
boydsmillspress.com

Printed in China

ISBN: 978-1-63592-142-7 (hc)
ISBN: 978-1-63592-363-6 (eBook)

Library of Congress Control Number: 2019940978

First edition

10 9 8 7 6 5 4 3 2

Book Design: Caitlin Greer
Calligraphy: Jane K. Estantino

Let's Dance!

WRITTEN BY VALERIE BOLLING   ILLUSTRATED BY MAINE DIAZ

BOYDS MILLS PRESS

AN IMPRINT OF BOYDS MILLS & KANE

New York

Fingers Snap

Turn, Twirl

Twist, Whirl

ZiG-ZaG-ZiG

SPIN, DIP, DIP

GROOViTY-GROOVe

Up on Toes

Strike a Pose

fall asleep

counting Sheep

Flamenco is from Southern Spain. Flamenco dancers clap their hands, snap their fingers, and stomp their feet.

Kathak is a dance from India. Kathak dancers tell stories with the movements of their hands and their jingling feet.

Irish Stepdancers must hold their bodies straight and move their feet quickly. Some Irish Stepdancers enjoy participating in dance competitions.

The Long-Sleeve Dance is from China. These dancers glide with long, flowing sleeves that move like water!

Kuku dancers jump high, dip low, and spin. This high-energy dance is from Guinea, West Africa.

The Cha-cha gets its name from the sound of the dancers' feet as they shuffle across the floor. This dance was invented in Cuba.

African-American youth created Breakdancing. Breakdancers can do amazing stunts, like handstands and headspins!

Line dance is done in a group. Line dancers practice doing the same steps all at the same time!

Disco dancers move all parts of their body at once—hands, head, and hips. This dance can be done alone or with a partner.

Ballet dancers move across the stage on their toes. When they leap, they fly through the air.